Bullet to the Brain

Marc Arginteanu

D1519611

1

Chapter One

The Expert Witness

Watanabe, the District Attorney, strutted like a rooster, back and forth, back and forth, across the worn marble tiles. "So," he said to the witness, "do you believe that the bullet, which Doctor Hoenniker dug out of the victim's brain, was shot from the semi-automatic Glock pistol the police found crammed in the defendant's pocket?"

Watanabe, though speaking to the ballistics expert, kept his eyes glued to the jury. When he said the words, 'dug out of the victim's brain,' a pencil-necked man in the second row of the jury box cringed and a satisfied smirk tugged at the corners of Watanabe's lips.

The middle-aged witness, who looked more like a librarian than a forensic expert, gripped the oaken parapet, as if to steady herself. She tried to avoid looking at the defendant, Tom Joad. But something about the man kept drawing her eyes back. She gulped and answered Watanabe's question with an ever so slight nod.

"The witness is required to provide the jury with a verbal response," the judge instructed.

Joad's eyes, a born predator's eyes, were locked upon the expert witnesses' jugulars. His jaw muscles clenched and unclenched, clenched and unclenched, keeping the rhythm of a tiger's swaying tail.

"Yes," the ballistics expert answered in a frightened squeak. She gazed about, desperately seeking an escape route.

"And what degree of certainty," Watanabe said. He studied the jury. He barked at the court reporter, "Strike that." He strutted back and forth, back and forth. His dark eyes twinkled, mischievously. "Just how sure are you that the slug, which blew through that poor boy's skull, whizzed through the barrel of the defendant's gun."

Watanabe had made the word 'defendant' sound a lot like 'scumbag.'

"Objection, Your Honor," the defense attorney said, jumping to his feet.

"Sustained."

"No further questions," Watanabe said. He leaned over the prosecutor's table and jotted some notes on his yellow pad. He was my age, thirty-eight, but looked at least five years younger than me. I guess it's the difference between eating right, sleeping well and getting regular exercise versus living on greasy cheeseburgers and bourbon and crawling into bed at sunrise. Or maybe it's just all in the genes.

"Nothing on cross," the defense attorney said.

"The witness may step down," the judge instructed.

"The prosecution calls Doctor Felix Hoenniker to the stand."

I stood up.

The girl beside me, Cady Compson, gripped my hand. She swished her silky, fragrant hair and gazed up at me. She didn't give a fig whether the whole world was waiting. She was going to hold my hand for as long as she felt like holding it. Her sloe eyes sparkled. Those eyes. They were the same shape (the color, though, was as different as night and day) as her baby brother's eyes. The dead brother. The brother from whose brain I'd dug the bullet.

"Doctor," the bailiff said impatiently. He held open the half-height swinging door, which led to the witness stand, with one hand. He beckoned to me with the crooked index finger of his other hand.

"Justice," Cady said to me through ripe-berry lips. Her voice was as hard as diamond. She squeezed my hand until it hurt, then dropped it.

After some preliminaries, Watanabe asked, "So, you're the neurosurgeon." His back was turned to the jury, so he treated me to a full sneer.

I must admit, I don't look the part. What, with my perpetual stubble and that ruby stud poking through my left earlobe and all.

Watanabe composed his features for the jurors and resumed his strut. "You're the neurosurgeon, who operated on Quentin Compson's brain." He locked eyes with a juror who was dozing off. He didn't let her off the hook until she sat up so straight that she looked like she would levitate off her seat. "You tried to save the poor boy. He was brought into Metro General with a gunshot to the head?"

"Yes."

"But there was no saving him?"

"No."

"And he didn't die right away, did he?"

"No," I said.

The defendant, aka scumbag killer, aka Tom Joad locked his eyes on me. His eyes said, 'Be careful up there, Doc. I've got a cousin who'll carve you up and float you down the Hudson, piece by piece.'

I met those cold eyes and my smirk asked, 'Why'd they slap that teardrop tattoo on your cheek, Tommy Boy? For creeping up behind a defenseless kid in an alley, putting a gun to his head and blowing his brains out? Or maybe it was because you took it up the butt at Riker's from some guy named Otto.'

"No peace for young Mr. Compson," Watanabe lugubriously shook his head. "Young, young Quentin. He was just eighteen years old. He lingered on for weeks in a coma, like a rotting vegetable."

"Your Honor!" The defense attorney jumped to his feet again.

"The prosecuting attorney *will* tone down the theatrics," the judge said.

"Young Quentin. With tubes and lines sticking in and out of every orifice," Watanabe said. "Would you agree, Doctor Hoenniker, that a dog shouldn't suffer like that?"

"Objection."

"Sustained. The jury will disregard that last question."

"What would you say, Doctor, was the cause of Quentin Compson's death?"

"A bullet to the brain."

"And you removed the bullet during brain surgery, in your heroic attempt to save Quentin's life." Watanabe had the jury hanging on his every word. They feared him, as if he were a fire and brimstone preacher who was weighing the merits of their souls. "Doctor, would you be able to identify the bullet if it were presented to you?"

"Yes."

"And you'd be certain."

"Yes."

"Please explain to the ladies and gentlemen of the jury how you'd be so sure."

"Well," I said. "I'm a neurosurgeon at a level one trauma center." My eyes wandered over the faces of the men and women in the jury. "And with the crime rate skyrocketing, I get pretty regular calls for gunshots to the head." I could tell they liked me. Juries always like me. "This is not my first rodeo. When I end up on the witness stand, I need to be able to definitively identify a particular bullet I've removed from a victim's brain." A few of the jurors were nodding. "So, I make a unique mark on each bullet before I send it down to the pathology department."

"This has been entered into evidence as P-1." Watanabe strutted over to the prosecutor's table. He snapped his fingers impatiently and his assistant handed him a Ziploc bag.

Watanabe's face, usually pasty, was flushed with excitement. I'd seen that look before. I've got a thumb drive in a drawer in my kitchen, where I keep all the other junk. There's a video of Watanabe, in a compromising position. A friend of mine secretly recorded it for me. I have lots of friends who aren't doctors.

Watanabe proffered the Ziploc bag.

I took it with a flourish and made a show of examining the bullet for the jury. I held it up to the light and squinted and everything. Someone should give me an Emmy.

After a few seconds, an icy chill shot through my guts.

In a tone that shouted, 'I live for this,' Watanabe asked, "Doctor Hoenniker, can you identify this bullet for the jury?"

"This isn't the bullet," I croaked.

"What?" Watanabe said and the color drained from his face.

"This is not the bullet I dug out of Quentin Compson's brain." I said.

The men and women of the jury gasped in unison, like the chorus in a Greek tragedy.

"It must have been a different bullet that killed Quentin."

A little while later, I climbed down from the witness stand and walked back to my seat. Cady stood up. She rose to the tips of her toes. She spat in my face. "Liar," she said and walked away.

"I'll make it right," I said. "I swear."

Cady shot poison tipped arrows from her eyes as she left the courtroom.

Rivulets of spittle slithered down my cheek like snails. "Damn," I said as I wiped the slime away with the sleeve of my jacket. "I just got this suit dry cleaned."

Soon after, Watanabe caught up to me in the hallway. "Felix," he said. "I know you hate me, but perjury?"

"Sure," I said. "Everything's got to be about you."

"Always a clever retort," he scoffed. He shook his finger in my face. A wagging finger felt better than spit, I guess. Unless you know where that finger's been. "Lying under oath is a felony. I'm going to see that this little performance costs you your medical license."

I walked out of the courthouse and turned my collar up to keep the rain from running down my neck. My feet led me towards Azazel's, a little hole in the wall that stocked Blanton's, my favorite bourbon. I would have loved to lie on the stand. There wasn't a doubt in my mind: that scumbag Tom Joad was guilty as hell. But I couldn't bring myself to do it. Bearing false witness was the only one of the ten commandments that I hadn't yet broken. If I could hold the line on that one, maybe I still had a shot at heaven.

"But," I asked the falling rain, "who switched the bullet?"

Chapter Two

Whiskey Chaser

Azazel's might look like a real dive, but it's got a lot going

for it. For one thing, I never need to order a double; the bartender

pours with a heavy hand. As a matter of fact, I never need to order at

all. Holly always knows what I need.

I glided over to the bar. Before I finished shaking the rain off

my coat and parking my narrow ass on a splintery stool, a tumbler

full of Blanton's appeared before me.

"Thanks Holly," I said.

She didn't answer. She'd already sailed halfway down the

bar and was pouring rot-gut tequila (with a shriveled sliver of lime)

for the only other guy in the place: a droopy figure in ill-fitting

clothes. Whenever I saw Holly from this angle, I heard the *Ride of

the Valkyries* playing in my head. She had porcelain skin and high

cheekbones. And man-oh-man was she buxom. What's more, blonde

braids hung halfway down her broad back.

When I was three-quarters through my bourbon, Bartleby appeared next to me and said, "Jeez! Were you brought up in a barn or something?" He grabbed my tumbler with his left hand and held it aloft. "This here bar is a thing of beauty." Using his right sleeve, he wiped away the wet ring, which had dripped from my tumbler. "They don't make 'em like this no more." He laid my bourbon down on the coaster. "Just look at the grain." The bar shone and was as smooth as black ice. "Wood like this can tell a story."

"I'm in the company of a real connoisseur," I said.

"I know what good is," he replied and slid over a manila envelope.

I peeled the Benjamins from my wad. Slowly, because I loved to watch the anticipation building in Bartleby's face. One, two, three, four, five, six. I slid them over and they disappeared, lickety-split, into his pocket.

"Can I get you anything, baby?" Holly asked Bartleby.

"It's ten in the morning," he protested.

She smiled at him.

The sadness in her sky-blue eyes blanketed me like a mist and made it a little hard to breathe. The Wagner music in my head ground to a screeching halt. Those eyes revealed what she really was: an angel whose wings had been clipped. "It's five o'clock somewhere."

I unclasped the envelope and dumped the thumb drive into my palm. "I hope there's something on here I can use, Bartleby."

"Have I ever let you down before?"

The last time I'd hired Bartleby, he saved me a bundle on the divorce. After seven long years, my wife had kicked me out. She said I was emotionally distant, or some shit like that. I don't remember her exact words because I wasn't really listening. She'd hired a hotshot lawyer to squeeze my nuts in a vice. Bartleby did a little surveillance and... what do you know? My Ex and the hotshot lawyer, who turned out to be Watanabe (the District Attorney who was now gunning for my medical license) were going hot and heavy on *my* four-poster king-sized bed. The weird part is, when I watched the video, my eager eye kept wandering back to him.

"You know, I hate spying on cops," Bartleby said. "What do you got against that crew anyways?"

"Nothing," I said. "Never even met a one of them."

I'd hired Bartleby to spy on three NYPD officers. They covered the shifts in the evidence room, down at the 123d Precinct House. I needed to figure out who'd swiped the bullet (which I'd dug out of Quentin Compson's brain) and replaced it with an unmarked slug. I hoped the trail started on Bartleby's thumb drive.

"Then what gives?"

"I made a promise to a lady," I said. "And I always keep my word."

I emptied my bourbon and saw Cady's face floating in the bottom of the glass. Tom Joad had slain her baby brother; over a stinking wallet; twenty-nine measly dollars. And now, because of *my* testimony, the scumbag was as free as a bird.

I plugged Bartleby's thumb drive into a USB-to-USB-C adapter and linked the adapter into my phone. I scrolled through the images. I bet that Bartleby could dig up dirt on anyone. Hell, even Mother Teresa must have some dirty laundry.

But there's dirt and then there's dirt.

Officer number one had the typical dirt. A wife and kids at home and a sweet little something on the side. The footage was nowhere near as raunchy as the video of my Ex and Watanabe. I snapped a few screenshots anyway.

Officer number two was a bit dirtier. Bartleby tailed him after he'd had one too many. Amongst other peccadilloes, he'd swerved his car into a row of parked cars, left a trail of broken side view mirrors on the pavement, and just drove away, laughing like a lunatic.

Officer number three was filthy. After perusing some of his hijinks, I marked him as just the kind of guy who'd be willing to take a bribe and let someone switch out evidence. Even if that meant a scumbag killer like Tom Joad would walk.

"I've got a hunch that this is my guy," I told Bartleby.

"I'd lay down money at three to one on any of your hunches," he said. "Officer Friendly spends his Tuesday nights at Xcess."

"Great," I said. "I happen to be in the mood to watch some pole dancing."

###

I kept my eye on officer number three. But I'm no fool. I wasn't going anywhere near him without Carmine.

I sipped on rot-gut whiskey. I know better than to order the top shelf stuff at a place like Xcess. You never really know what you're going to get; they just fill the bottle with any old crap and switch the label. What's more, they water down everything.

I treated myself to a few lap dances, though. I didn't want to blow my cover. And besides, unlike the booze, the girls at Xcess are always top notch.

Carmine sauntered in, fifteen minutes before closing time. Now, I'm long and lean. Carmine… Well, he's a head taller than me and twice as wide. He looks as soft as a Botero painting, but he's as solid as an oak tree.

"Drink?" I asked.

"Not when I'm working," he said. That was his little hint. So, I peeled two Benjamins from my wad and slapped them into his eager palm.

The girl, who was gyrating on my lap, noticed the transfer of green. She asked him, "Looking for a girlfriend?"

"Not when I'm working," Carmine answered.

I was the beneficiary of a steep discount on Carmine's services. A few years prior, a gang of slime balls had shoved his grandma down the subway stairs and cracked three vertebrae in her neck. I had to use twice the usual number of screws to get her neck all fixed up, because her old-lady bones were soft as butter and crumbly as blue cheese. I also helped him track down the thugs. I have lots of friends who aren't doctors.

After the closing bell rang, we followed the filthy cop out to the parking lot. Carmine threw him up against his SUV and said, "Now, you're gonna tell the good doctor all what he wants to know."

"Or what?" He said and reached for his pistol.

But Carmine is as fast as a cobra. He grabbed the gun and slapped it on the roof of the cop's car. "Or I'm gonna punch you in the face."

I asked the filthy cop who switched the evidence.

He answered with a scoff.

I nodded to Carmine.

Carmine punched him in the face.

After the cop woke up and wiped the blood from his face, I asked him again.

"I don't know," he answered.

I nodded to Carmine.

Carmine punched him in the face.

After the cop woke up, I handed him his front two teeth and said, "Maybe you can stick these under the pillow, I hear the tooth fairy is very generous in your neighborhood."

"Fuck you," he spat.

I didn't want Carmine to bruise up his knuckles too much. I never know when I'll need his services. So, I stuck my phone in the cop's face and played one of Bartleby's videos.

"Who switched the bullet?" I asked.

"Nick Caraway," he said.

"You mean Dr. Caraway?"

He nodded.

"Holy shit," I said. Nick Caraway was one of my oldest friends. We'd gone to medical school together. "Why the hell would he do that?"

Chapter Three

With Friends Like These

I've probably visited my good old buddy, Nick Caraway, at work a hundred times. But even if I visit a thousand times more, I'll never get used to the smell. The only way I can stand it is by dripping benzoin into the center of two cotton balls and sticking one fluffy ball up each nostril.

"Felix," Nick said, a big smile painted across his face, a fat cigar (its tip aglow) clenched between his teeth.

"Nick," I said, holding a bottle aloft.

My Spidey senses should've started to tingle when I set down the eighteen-year-old bottle of Laphroaig and all he gave back was a fading smile and cool, "Thank you." He usually gushes over a bottle like that, which would be tough to swing on a coroner's salary.

"You want to give me a hand with this?" He asked. "It's right up your alley."

Nick was doing an autopsy on a thirty-ish year-old guy who'd died after crescendoing episodes of psychosis and mental decline. The differential diagnoses were drug induced mental deterioration versus Mad Cow Disease.

Nick used a fierce looking circular saw to cut out a piece of the guy's skull, about the size of a soup bowl. Then, he scooped out his brain. It wasn't an untreated brain, which would have oozed out of his head like swamp-mud this far post-mortem. It was preserved in formaldehyde, so it had a firm, putty-like consistency. The brain came out in one big chunk and its extraction made the slurp-sucking sound of a plunger being yanked from a toilet bowl. Then, Nick sliced the cerebrum like a loaf of bread.

"Multiple hemorrhages," I observed. He'd laid out the brain slices in orderly rows and columns across his examining table. "Hypertensive pattern."

"Yeah," he agreed. "Cocaine induced."

"Too bad," I said. "Mad Cow is so much more... horror show."

Nick scoffed and shook his head.

"Do you mind if we go into your office?" I asked, feeling a little queasy and looking green around the gills. "You can fill out the death certificate there. I've got a couple of questions I've got to ask you."

"Sure, sure." He peeled off his latex gloves and shot them, like rubber bands, into the trash. "You've got no stomach for the perfume of the dead," he laughed. "You always were a bit of a snowflake." He puffed his cigar and we walked out of the morgue.

The smell of rotting flesh and bursting bowels is awful enough. But what really got to me was the cloying smell of formaldehyde: it seeped into my pores whenever I stood at the autopsy table and percolated out of my skin for days afterwards.

I pushed a finger against each side of my nose and shot the cotton balls from my nostrils. They struck the aluminum trash can and clanged like cowbells. "Ahh," I said and settled into the dilapidated sofa. It's not like Nick's office smelled like a rose garden, but at least I could inhale without gagging.

He snuffed out his cigar and poured us a couple of drinks.

The second hint (which, like the first, I ignored) there was something rotten in the state of Denmark was the major upgrade to Nick's scotch collection. He pulled a twenty-five-year-old bottle of Laphroaig from the cabinet and relegated my eighteen-year-old gift to the shadowy depths.

"The usual?" Nick asked.

"Unless you've seen the light and started to stock bourbon."

He scoffed. He poured out two fingers of eighteen-year-old Oban and handed me the glass.

I appreciate single malt scotch, of course, but I always go for Highland (like Oban). The Islay (like Laphroaig) Nick jizzes over, turns my stomach. The peaty flavor tastes like formaldehyde to me, as if I'm drinking cadaver juice.

We raised our glasses and toasted our old med school days.

"To the valedictorian," I said.

"To the runner up," he smirked.

After two sips the room started spinning.

"Felix, Felix, Felix," Nick said, "I knew that *you* knew when I saw that bottle in your hand." He shook his head regretfully. "Eighteen-year-old Laphroaig… that's Christmas or birthday scotch."

The glass fell from my hand. It shattered on the tiled floor. "Why would you protect a scumbag killer like Tom Joad?"

"Why?" He scoffed. "Because I'm tired of parking my beat-up old Ford next to your Porsche."

"Just for the money?" I slurred. My whole body was tingling and my limbs felt like lead.

"Easy for you to say, Felix." His thumbs danced across his cell phone as he sent a text message. "I bust my ass day after day; carving up cadavers, writing reports, answering to administrators who aren't fit to tie my shoes."

"And you? You come and go like the wind. You charge Metro General fifteen hundred bucks a day." An offended expression (the injustice of the universe) crossed his face. "Fifteen hundred bucks! Just to carry around a stinking beeper and prance in like a rockstar when a neurotrauma rolls in."

"I'd call it more of a strut than a prance." I was drooling. I slumped over sideways.

"You should've stuck to your day job," he scoffed, "instead of making like you're some sort of Sherlock Holmes."

Tom Joad and another goon burst through the door. One grabbed my left arm, the other my right and they yanked me from the sofa. My head lolled and my legs dragged behind as they hauled me across Nick's office and through the labyrinthine basement of Metro General. The last thing I remember is being tossed (like a sack of potatoes) into their white van.

When I woke up, my head throbbed like a blister ready to burst. My eyes drifted into focus and locked onto a squat figure stalking, back and forth, back and forth, like a penned-up wolf. I blinked a few more times and saw the Manhattan skyline beyond him, through floor-to-ceiling windows. It was a foggy night and the lights from all the skyscrapers melted together like ice-cream.

Though the buildings were on the other side of the Hudson, they seemed close enough to touch.

My host was dressed for the cover of GQ; he even had one of those little handkerchiefs (which matched his socks) peeking from his jacket pocket. He bent his globular head and watched a ferry load up on passengers; nighttime revelers headed to the heart of Gotham. His square face wore a sneer, as if every last one of them ought to be paying him a toll for breathing *his* air.

"You're Joseph Kurtz," I said, recognizing him from frequent cameos on *Page Six* of *The New York Post*.

"Guilty as charged," he said. He sat down across from me on a suede chair (which matched the seat in which I slumped) and refilled his glass from an elegant decanter. He held the wine aloft. "Hair of the dog?"

I figured it was my last drink. So, I said, "I'd take a bourbon, neat. Blanton's, if you've got it. Hold the Rohypnol."

Kurtz nodded and someone handed me a drink. Kurtz rested his Gucci shod feet on the mahogany table, which separated us. He lifted his glass (his ruby-red wine sloshing) towards the skyline, "That view never gets old."

"I'm more the outerboro type, myself." The whiskey eased my headache. "Manhattan has too many assholes… I guess some of you moved to New Jersey."

Kurtz laughed.

I sipped my bourbon. It wasn't Blanton's but it was very fine. I tried not to think about whether Kurtz was going to kill me quickly or slowly. But my mind kept drifting back to Quentin Compson and how he lingered in a coma for weeks and weeks. I said, "Do me one favor."

Kurtz raised his eyebrows.

"If I'm getting a bullet in the brain, do the job right."

"You're not very bright for a brain surgeon," he said. "If I wanted you dead, I wouldn't have wasted the Pappy van Winkle."

I sipped the bourbon with a new appreciation.

"I'll wager you're wondering why I'd go through so much trouble… tampering with evidence, kidnapping a neurosurgeon… for a cretin like Tom Joad."

"Birds of a feather?"

"You're closer than you think." Kurtz laughed. "Joad was one of my bodyguards until he started showing up to work high as a kite. Rather than give him the sack, I flipped his job description. Something more in line with his proclivities. He became a guinea pig for our new line of inhalable drugs. They work with JUUL vaporizers, by the way. In my business, you've got to change with the fashion to remain relevant."

I lifted my empty Waterford crystal tumbler and an invisible hand poured me a refill. Unfortunately, Kurtz's man was not as heavy handed as Holly.

"Anyway," Kurtz continued. "I became a touch too curious and stepped in a tad too close. Joad exhaled a big cloud of mist and I sucked it down to the depths of my lungs. When I next looked in the mirror, my eye color had changed."

I sat forward. "Hmm." I shone my cell phone light at Kurtz's face. It was as if I were on the witness stand again, looking at that scumbag sitting at the defense table. "Those are Joad's eyes!"

"Bingo," Kurtz said. "And that's just the beginning... Have you ever heard of quantum entanglement?"

I wondered whether this conversation was really happening. Maybe the Pappy was spiked, too. It tasted so good that it didn't matter. I took another sip and answered, "Subatomic particles, despite being separated by vast distances, can change each other's properties, an effect that moves faster than the speed of light."

"Close enough," Kurtz said. "Well, that designer drug entangled our life forces; mine and Joad's. So, if he dies, so do I."

"So, you sprung him from Ryker's to protect your own skin."

"I've heard it said that a lot of nasty shit goes down in prison."

"Especially if your name is Jeffrey Epstein."

He laughed.

I shook my head in wonder. "Quantum entanglement designer drugs."

A burly dude set a plate of cheese, which smelled like sweaty feet, upon the table.

"I know, I know," Kurtz said, noting my crinkled nose. "But it pairs divinely with the wine." He savored some food and drink and then said, "You might imagine that I'm not thrilled to be entangled with anyone, least of all a cretin like Joad. Unfortunately, the lady who synthesized the entanglement drug ran off when she caught wind of my displeasure."

"So," I asked. "Why am I still breathing?"

"You, my friend, are like a lemon," he answered. "You've got a lot of juice yet."

"And you're going to squeeze. But where, exactly, do I fit in?"

"You are going to fetch my little chemist. My associates caught up to her in Prague. I need someone with a squeaky-clean passport, such as an esteemed physician, who won't raise any eyebrows at customs, to toodle over there and escort her back… And don't even think about getting cute. Until you get back here, Joad's going to be sticking to your little girlfriend like shit to a shovel."

"She's not my girlfriend anymore," I said and a wistful smile crossed my face. "She's joined the long line of my Ex's." I drowned a little sorrow with a gulp of Pappy. "Her choice, not mine."

Cady Compson… The sweet perfume of her silky hair filled my nostrils and the angry taste of her spit filled my mouth.

I'll make it right, Cady. I swear.

Chapter Four

Fetching the Chemist

I strolled around and around the little plaza (my eighth lap) wondering if the chemist would ever show up. "Well, it's a nice day, anyway," I said to myself. And it really was nice. The neat rows of azalea bushes, which bordered the square, were in full bloom. Each cluster of color was a fluffy little puff of Prague's springtime.

The imposing sculpture in the center of the plaza was weird, but it had a good vibe. An immense, empty bronze suit strode across a disc-like pedestal. A well-dressed man straddled the empty suit's shoulders, like a horse and rider. The man's expression (his eyes and mouth couldn't seem to agree) shifted depending on how the light and shadow struck him; now smirking; now forlorn; now seeking. He pointed an accusatory finger directly at me. I bent forward and read the name engraved upon the pedestal, "Franz Kafka."

An icy hand clutched my shoulder and I leapt half out of my skin.

"Guilty conscience?" Addie Bundren asked.

"Being sent to a foreign land by a sleazy drug dealer makes me a little jumpy," I said. "You scared the shit out of me."

She had a piercing gaze and her close-cropped hair clung, disconcertingly, to her scalp.

"You must be the chemist," I said.

"You must be the chaperone," she said.

"Felix Hoenniker," I stuck out my hand.

"I was informed I'd be traveling in the company of an esteemed physician." She left my hand hanging in the warm spring breeze. "Forgive me, but…" Her eyes, each one a different color, roamed over my stubbly cheeks and rumpled clothes. She grimaced, as if something bitter filled her mouth and she'd no option but to swallow. "Well," she sighed, "at least you have intelligent eyes."

"What's with giving me the runaround this morning?" My voice sounded bitchier than I'd intended. I cleared my throat to banish the peevish tone. "If I knew I was getting a scenic tour of the old city, I'd have worn comfortable shoes." We'd been scheduled to meet right after breakfast. She'd texted me five times, changing the time and location.

"I needed to make sure you weren't being followed by Kurtz's men," Addie said. Her eyes narrowed and she asked, "Are you here of your own volition?"

I explained how Kurtz had sicced Tom Joad on Cady Compson.

"Ah, yes. Kurtz holds the sword of Damocles over my head as well." Addie explained how Joad was sticking to her daughter, D.D. (a college student at New York University) like shit to a shovel.

"So, Kurtz grabbed us both by the short hairs," I observed. "Why did you run away from him?"

"Kurtz," she scoffed. "That egotistical pissant. He imagines the world revolves around him. No, no, it's not from him I was running. I fled something far more sinister: the voice."

"Voice?" I asked.

"The voice in my head." Addie shuddered. "The voice doesn't compel me outright. But he can be quite persuasive."

Well, I guess that's why she needed a chaperone. She had a screw loose.

"I designed drugs for Kurtz because I needed funding. The pharmaceutical industry can be so… so… stodgy. I endeavored to fabricate a substance, which might snuff out the voice, once and for all."

Judging by the frenetic cadence of her speech and the wild gleam of her eyes, she must've sampled one too many of her own creations.

"Where science failed," Addie said. "Love succeeded." She undid the top three buttons of her paisley blouse. "D.D. made this for me, with her own hands." She displayed a delicate silver necklace, which glimmered against her buttery skin. "As soon as it contacted my flesh, that horrid voice was silenced." The chain links were simple and unadorned, but elegant. "Please, check whether the clasp is secure." She turned her back towards me and bent her long, slender neck forwards. "I'm terrified of it becoming undone."

At the intersection of her shoulder, back and neck was a tattoo: arcane symbols and letters from a long-forgotten tongue cast in twisting, intertwining, concentric circles...

I've seen that emblem before. But where?

The design sucked me towards a faraway world......

That's where I've seen it! It's carved into the door of my favorite bar, Azazel's Public House.

I spun slowly under a dark, starless sky, floating in a warm ocean...........

"Whoa!" I said and leapt half out of my skin.

Addie had stuck her icy hands underneath my shirt. Her palms ran up, down and around my torso. Before I knew it, she reached inside my shorts and (none too gently) groped around.

"Hey! You could at least buy a guy a drink first."

"Excellent, excellent, no wires," Addie said. "Now, give me your phone."

I handed it over.

She tossed it into an azalea bush.

"Hey!"

"I don't fancy Siri's eavesdropping," she explained. "Listen closely: Kurtz is threatening my dear D.D.. Needless to say, he's on my naughty list now. We have very little time to devise a plan."

###

A pair of Kurtz's goons were waiting for Addie and me when we landed at Newark Airport. They whisked us off: long black limousine to forty-foot boat at the mouth of the Passaic River. Addie tossed crumbs and laughed; starving seagulls squawked and battled each other for a bite to eat. In the crisp sunlight, her hair (which hugged her scalp in tight curls) glistened like a dewy field. When she caught me staring, her expression grew haughty.

The river twisted and turned, deeper and deeper into the heart of New Jersey. We chugged along; afternoon gave way to evening and the fat, red sun sunk low over the Watchung Mountains.

We disembarked in a rural county, surrounded by rolling hills and horse farms. A winding path snaked from the muddy banks of the Passaic towards a ghostly-white Greek Revival mansion. Along the path, hidden speakers piped orchestral arrangements of seventies disco tunes. "The elevator music from hell," I observed.

"Kurtz! That rascal knows this melody melts my heart," Addie said. "Yes, yes, he's quite the charmer. But I've seen behind the curtain." She shook her head, as if to banish the Siren's song. She repeated to herself, "Stick to the plan, stick to the plan, stick to the plan…"

I shushed her when Kurtz came into view. He stood before a built-in grill in the center of the vast stone patio. He wore a pristine white apron, which protected his bespoke blue blazer and butt-hugging khakis. He bobbed his globular head and hummed along with the softly playing tunes. When he spotted us, he said, "Ah, you must be famished." He speared a steak (generously marbled with fat) with a two-tined fork. "Wagyu."

He tenderly spread the meat over the dancing flames.

The tantalizing aroma (oh, so good) soon had my mouth dripping.

"It will take more than a choice cut of beef to get yourself back onto my nice list," Addie said. "Where's my daughter?"

"All in good time, my dear," Kurtz said. "All in good time."

"I demand—"

"We both know, Addie, that you're in no more a position to make demands than the good doctor. You'll see D.D. and Felix will be reunited with his paramour… after you concoct a potion to disentangle me from that cretin, Joad."

Rage bubbled under Addie's skin. She breathed deeply and battled against herself for a long moment. The boiling settled down to a simmer. "The voyage has been long," she said, wearily.

"Travel is a curse," he replied. "Why don't you toodle up to your room." He waved a shooing hand. "Freshen up a bit and change into something more comfortable."

Figuring this was likely my last meal, I wolfed down a couple of pounds of the best steak I'd ever eaten (like butter in my mouth); all the better for having been masterfully paired with a garnet-red, earthy Malbec. I was so stuffed I barely found the gastric capacity for dessert: golden sponge cake soaked in honey, which had been harvested from a beehive on Kurtz's property. "Kurtz," I said. "If you weren't a sleazy drug dealer, you'd be far and away the coolest dude I know."

Kurtz only had eyes for Addie, "Don't pretend you didn't miss me a little, my dear."

Addie's unfocused eyes told me the fine wine had gone to her head. "You wouldn't have harmed her?"

"D.D.?" Kurtz smiled and spread his arms wide. "Perish the thought. You know she's like a daughter to me."

"Don't sharks eat their young?" I said.

Kurtz didn't find my jibes as amusing as the first time we'd met. Stirring estrogen into the mix usually has that effect.

A woodwind and string arrangement of The Bee Gees song, *More than a Woman,* filled the night air. An enchanted smile played on Addie's lips. She reached a slender arm out to Kurtz, "Shall we?"

Kurtz extended his hand and pulled Addie to her feet. She was clad in Lululemon athleisure wear and spiked high heels. With those stilettos on her feet, she gazed slightly downwards into his eyes. They spun across the patio as gracefully as John Travolta and Karen Gorney in *Saturday Night Fever*. Kurtz wrapped a beefy paw around Addie's narrow waist and drew her in, close and tight. She lay her head on his shoulder.

She winked at me. She held up five fingers on her right hand and three on her left.

I nodded.

Chapter Five

Tangled up with Addie

After thoroughly enjoying a shit, shower and shave, I was

guided (by a goon) through a maze of elephant tusk archways into

Kurtz's office. Kurtz leaned back in a fur lined chair, which was

upholstered with the hide of a poor beast he'd poached on safari. His

Gucci shod feet rested on the ponderous desk; a nineteenth century

antique; rosewood, inlaid with mother of pearl.

"Nightcap?" He asked.

I nodded.

Kurtz opened an ornate cabinet, which was the same vintage

as the desk, and pulled out a decanter. He poured two fingers of

bourbon for me (and three for himself) into Waterford crystal

tumblers. I held mine up, "To my surviving the night."

"Ah, my dear Felix. Where does one draw the line between optimism and self-delusion?" He asked.

My smile faltered.

To my relief, he lifted his glass and laughed. The light filtered through the amber whiskey and was refracted into dancing rainbows by the heavy, heavy, hand cut crystal.

Addie walked in (flushed with excitement) wearing a white lab coat. She'd changed her stilettos for sensible shoes. She'd forgotten to remove her safety goggles; a layer of fog made her two eyes appear the same, nondescript, color.

"Ah, my sweet chemist," Kurtz said with a condescending smile. He tapped his temple.

Her excited flush deepened to an embarrassed blush. For a moment I saw the teenage girl she'd been; awkward and nerdy and perpetually mocked by the cool kids. She removed the goggles and tossed them aside; the poise returned to her posture; the panache rushed back to her face; her eyes regained their vibrant David-Bowie-colors.

My heart leapt.

"Have you met with success?" Kurtz asked.

"I stand before you triumphant." Addie proffered a Ziplock bag full of cartridges, which were akin to JUUL pods. "I was on the verge of solving your life force entanglement quandary before I indulged in my little sabbatical."

"Excellent," Kurtz smiled.

"As a show of goodwill," Addie continued. "I also cooked up a big batch of Vardaman."

"Vardaman?" I asked.

"A cross between Molly and Special K," Kurtz explained. "The club kids have been going gaga over it."

"I sent a few of your boys down the river with a boatload," Addie said.

"A boatload?" Kurtz's smile grew toothy. "That should net a cool hundred grand. This calls for some Louis XIII."

As he rooted around the cabinet for a cognac snifter, Addie held up four fingers.

I nodded.

Kurtz proffered the Louis XIII to Addie. She turned up her nose. "I've held up my end of the bargain. I'll not share a drink, or anything else, with you until—"

The sturdy oak door creaked open. Joad shoved D.D. and Cady into Kurtz's office and followed closely at their heels.

"You were saying?" Kurtz smirked.

"Mom!" D.D. said and rushed Addie's loving embrace.

"I should have known *you* were somehow mixed up in all this," Cady hissed at me. Her narrowed eyes shot daggers and her gnashing teeth were ready to devour me (not in a good way).

"I hope you ladies will join us in a toast," Kurtz said. "Cognac? Bourbon? Or perhaps I should call for a bottle of Champagne?"

"Cady will have some whiskey," I said.

Cady opened her mouth to protest. But the words died in her throat. She seemed to be deciding which she loathed more, me or bourbon. The wheels spun for a moment. She finally said, "I take it neat."

"Let's get the formalities over with," Addie said. She handed a JUUL vaporizer to Joad.

"Not so fast," Kurtz said. He settled in behind his desk. "Joad, you and your charges will stand over there," he pointed, "by the bookcase."

Joad dragged D.D. and Cady to the far side of the room.

"My father, after he was shipped off to the federal penitentiary, had a little saying: Trust, but verify." Kurtz said. "A pity he'd not learned that lesson earlier in life." He shook his globular head contemplatively. "D.D., you'll be taking the first puff of your mother's latest concoction."

"You bastard," Addie said.

"Don't make me ask twice," Kurtz's voice was like ice.

Addie nodded to her daughter.

D.D. inhaled a mouthful.

"Do it like you mean it," Kurtz said.

D.D. inhaled a lungful, blew out a cloud of mist and repeated the cycle several times.

Kurtz poured himself another three fingers of Pappy. He put his feet up on the desk and sipped until his tumbler was empty. "How do you feel, my dear?" he asked D.D.

"A little tingly around the lips."

"Your turn, Joad," Kurtz said.

The scumbag killer inhaled long and deep.

"Pterion," I said to Cady.

She cocked her head and looked at me quizzically.

"Pterion," I repeated.

The lightbulb flashed in Cady's mind. She remembered the self-defense lesson, which (months earlier) I'd imparted to her. She swung the heavy, heavy crystal tumbler at Joad's head. The pterion is the weakest spot on the skull. The middle meningeal artery courses, like a subterranean river, right below. She struck him squarely on the spot.

Clunk.

Joad shook it off. His sneer said, 'I'm no stranger to street fights, you bitch.' He pulled his fist back to wallop Cady.

She cringed, closed her eyes and steeled herself for the blow.

Kurtz drank in the scene, a lurid smile painted on his square face.

Joad fell backwards.

Thud.

Kurtz fell sideways.

Thud.

"He wasn't shitting me," I said. "They were entangled, big time."

Addie's drug had not been designed to disentangle Joad's and Kurtz's life forces. It was designed to make the arteries in the inhaler's body as flimsy as wet toilet paper. Cady's blow had ruptured the middle meningeal artery in Joad's brain, which had caused a lethal epidural hemorrhage.

The drug was also designed to *only* affect cells housing 'Y' chromosomes. D.D.'s cells, of course, were full of 'X's'. Not a 'Y' in sight. Addie's nobody's fool.

"Ten Mississippi… Nine Mississippi…" Addie began the countdown. She locked the oaken door.

The four fingers (which Addie had held aloft when she stepped into Kurtz's office) indicated the number of armed men who remained on Kurtz's estate. Addie had held eight fingers aloft during the barbecue, but she'd sent four armed men down the river with the cache of Vardaman. Eight minus four equals four.

"Eight Mississippi… Seven Mississippi…"

I heaved and strained and flipped Kurtz's desk onto its side. I hoped the thick rosewood would protect us. Addie herded the girls over. We all huddled behind the fine antique.

"Six Mississippi… Five Mississippi…"

Of the four remaining armed men, two, Joad and Kurtz, were dead. Four minus two equals two live goons at the Kurtz estate.

Addie's countdown indicated the amount of time we had until those last two were upon us. "Four Mississippi... Three Mississippi..."

Just as she'd reckoned, the remaining two goons began shouting and pounding on the stout office door.

I ran my hands underneath Kurtz's bespoke blue blazer. Nothing but broad pecs and chiseled abs. "I thought you said he always carries a gun."

"Two Mississippi... Ankle holster... One Mississippi..."

I found the pistol strapped to his muscular calf.

Gunshots rang out. One of the goons shot out the lock. They kicked in the door and burst through.

As a neurosurgeon, I pride myself on my steady hands. But as I leveled the Sig at the goons, my hands shook and my heart fluttered like a candle in the wind. I held my breath and pulled the trigger.

Click.

"What the fuck?" I said.

"I thought you said you were an expert with firearms," Addie said.

"I never used the word 'expert'," I said.

The pair of goons wasted an extra few Mississippis. They gazed (open mouthed) at Joad, whose lifeless body was sprawled across the floor. One of them poked him with a toe.

I pulled the trigger again.

It didn't even 'click.'

The goons locked on our position and raised their pistols.

"The slide!" I chided myself. I yanked the slide back and released, chambering the first round.

The two goons and I all emptied our magazines.

Their bullets turned the fine antique desk into splinters.

My rounds turned the goons into Swiss cheese. Well, not exactly. Most of my twelve bullets turned Kurtz's books into confetti, the walls into sieves, the water pipes into fountains… you get the idea. But a couple of 9mms found their target and the goons lay dead.

When the dust settled, D.D. embraced her mother and said, "I knew you'd save me, Mom."

Cady slapped me real hard and said, "You've been nothing but a pox upon my family. If I never see you again, it will be too soon." She turned, stepped over the dead bodies and walked out of Kurtz's office. I hated to see her go, but I loved watching her lower unit recede down the hallway.

"Good luck getting an Uber out here, Cady," I said. I rubbed my stinging cheek and her palm print faded away.

"Use the G-Wagon," Addie told D.D.. "It should be parked behind the Lamborghini. Take that poor girl back home. By the time you return I'll have figured out the combination to Kurtz's safe and we'll skedaddle with a tidy sum."

Addie turned the piercing spotlight of her gaze towards me. "Felix, I trust you will give us a few hours head start before you alert the authorities."

"Take your time getting back here, D.D.," I said. "Addie, do me one favor before you skedaddle."

She raised her eyebrows.

"Strap those stilettos back on and teach me some of your fancy dance moves."

She extended her hand and I took it.

I hoped our little tango would be starting vertically and ending horizontally.

Made in the USA
Middletown, DE
17 December 2022